SEVERAL SHORT STORIES AND POEMS

SUE MACLAURIN

authorHOUSE

AuthorHouse™ UK
1663 Liberty Drive
Bloomington, IN 47403 USA
www.authorhouse.co.uk
Phone: UK TFN: 0800 0148641 (Toll Free inside the UK)
*   UK Local: (02) 0369 56322 (+44 20 3695 6322 from outside the UK)*

Published by AuthorHouse 08/17/2023

ISBN: 979-8-8230-8424-6 (sc)
ISBN: 979-8-8230-8425-3 (e)

Library of Congress Control Number: 2023915573

Print information available on the last page.

Any people depicted in stock imagery provided by Getty Images are models, and such images are being used for illustrative purposes only. Certain stock imagery © Getty Images.

This book is printed on acid-free paper.

CONTENTS

Poems

A LITTLE INFORMATION ABOUT ME

My motto is: Life is like an expensive Mystery Voyage, so keep positive and expect the best.

My words of advice, whatever happens, are:

1. Make the most of every day, helping other living beings and learning what you can.
2. We live in a peculiar age, where history and technology and bodies of all kinds are manipulated and reinvented, so think for yourself and do your best for yourself and others.
3. Remember your personal addresses! Because:

I was born in a village that is now becoming part of a town in England (aka Britain and UK), so technically nowadays I was not born anywhere.

I lived in Southern Rhodesia, Rhodesia, Zimbabwe/Rhodesia and Zimbabwe at various times. To give you all the place names means a lot more of the aka and I'm trying to keep this short. But when I was 9 to 14 years old I lived in Wankie; I went to boarding school in Bulawayo but lived during daylight hours mostly on the kopje outside our house or in the local swimming pool and I can't remember those addresses, but particularly wish I knew the Wankie one now.

I also lived in Ceylon (aka Sri Lanka) for a couple of years, mostly in a house, but where??

In case you're wondering: my late father was a peripatetic brickworks manager most of the time and my ex-husband was mostly a consulting civil engineer.

4. Do your best for babies everywhere – animal, vegetable and mineral (think of crystals) – as they have the ability to be and do wonderful things if tended and nurtured with love and loving care. I have four wonderful sons, who were born respectively in South Africa, Ceylon, Zimbabwe/Rhodesia, and Zimbabwe. They have me to thank for their dual nationalities and citizenship or not, and of course their wonderfulness.

5. Learn and study whenever you can. I made great use of all the free or fairly cheap courses I came across, whatever and wherever. I have all sorts of qualifications including a degree, and still use most of this knowledge. It's amazing what you can learn (e.g. CPR, sewing, cement mixing) and then use to help others.

6. Keep positive and keep going each day, and tell yourself that everything happens for a reason, even though things seem hopeless. Sometimes it's as though we're in an endless stormy sea of life, but believe me there is always a happy ending waiting for us at the end of our individual expensive mystery voyages.

TWINKLES AND THE GODDESS

Hot and sweet. Waves like a heartbeat. Durban!

"Go to the beach then," shouted her mother crossly. "See if I care!"

"You're so childish!" Twinkles shouted back, "And I know that you hate me too!"

"Of course I don't," her mother replied, slightly hoarse, "I don't, I don't, but I'm so sick of arguments and - and-"

Twinkles recognised an opportunity. "And I'm sick of you!" she yelled triumphantly. She slammed the door behind her as she left the house.

"And I can't cope anymore," Twinkles heard her mother wail behind her. Twinkles took off in true Olympic fashion, her long pale brown legs moving fast.

As she ran, she thought about the whole stinking mess of their shopping day. There was nothing in any shop at all, anywhere, that she could wear to the party. And there were so many clothes in the world! It didn't seem fair that everyone on the planet, except herself, was well-dressed and happy. And her mother had accused her of sulking. Sulking! She had sat under the T-shirt rail only because she was tired. And she had refused to move because she was sick of having nothing to wear. She could never go to the party now, and perhaps she would never go to a party again.

She gasped out loud as her feet plunged into the hot sand on the beach. With the road behind her, and the vast blueness of the sea and sky in front, she slowed down to a walk. She kicked up sprays of sand and started to cry. Her heart thumped wildly with anger and exertion. She put a hand on her breast and immediately thought of her mother, and a few famous singers. "Flat!" she shouted into the waves, "And it's not bloody fair!" And she quickly glanced up and down the beach to make sure that it was, in fact, deserted.

The sand stretched whitely, and the waves thumped and splashed. Two figures in the far distance were all that she could see.

With another fierce cry, she ripped her bikini top off. She was so under-developed that the top resembled a fattish ribbon attached to a few bits of meagre string. And she stood there in the sun, trembling with emotion.

They - everyone - kept telling her that she would "round out nicely" or something equally fatuous, given time. But how much time could they mean? She'd waited for thirteen years already! It was so frustrating, and her clothes remained so - flat. And now there was this party, and Mike was going to be there, and he was in the school play, and he was so-o-o handsome. He had blonde hair and green eyes and dark eyelashes that were so-o-o dreamy, and if she went to the party he might even look at her....

She stood there dreaming, absent-mindedly winding the bikini top around her head so that she looked like a blonde Red Indian brave. Her body was well-proportioned and slim, and her face was beautiful. She was at the age where both boys and girls still look almost sexless: smooth, perfect, new, as Adam and Eve must have looked before that fertile, infernal tree bore fruit.

"Mike!" she thought, "Mike, you are so fantastic, amazing..." And she jumped back in alarm as a figure rose up from the waves at her feet.

The woman, all curves and waist-length hair, wore a blue wet-suit. She looked at Twinkles with a strange expression, more with curiosity than with surprise. "Hallo there," she said in a musical voice.

"Erm, hallo", Twinkles answered, and added honestly, "You frightened me!"

"I'm sorry," said the woman. She stepped out of the water and stood between Twinkles and the moving sea. "Slivaak," she said, and then she wore a long dress that clung to her body, and sparkled and glittered around her as though the material was made of diamonds.

"Sheez!" Twinkles exclaimed, and sat abruptly in the sand.

"I beg your pardon?" the woman asked, politely enough. She looked fairly harmless, Twinkles thought. In fact, she looked quite nice, like a film star, or a goddess, or something.

"Yes," said the woman firmly. "That's quite right. I am a goddess".

Twinkles felt anxious. "You knew what I was thinking," she said. "Can you read minds or what?"

The woman frowned, "Can't you read minds?" she asked.

"Of course not!" Twinkles answered.

The woman raised a round box to her lips, and spoke into it, as though it was a 'phone. "Genetically inferior," said the goddess sadly. "But beautiful, more beautiful than I imagined the young of this race to be. That is a consolation. Those on Beta-9," she added, "Were everything we were looking for - they could even insalucidate upside-down, but they looked so grotesque that we became over-sensitive. All those superfluous tentacles...." she mused. She stopped talking into the box, and held it in her hand.

Twinkles was interested. "What does insalucidate mean?" she interupted.

The Goddess's cheeks became pinker. "Don't you know?" she asked incredulously.

Twinkles was aware that the two figures she had seen earlier, in the distance, were moving towards them. They were two muscular young men, carrying surf boards.

"Far out, George," she heard one say. "Check the dumpers!"

Twinkles scrambled up, out of the clinging sand, and ran over to them.

The Goddess stood quietly, more lovely than the most expensive lady in any television advertisement.

"Look!" Twinkles said to the two men, "A Goddess!"

"Yeah," said the man who continued to admire the large waves, and merely glanced in a disinterested way at her. And he addressed his companion again. "What do you think, George?"

George appeared to think hard. "The barrels will be rolling in at Anstey's," he said at last. "What do you say, Tommy?"

"You surfers have got one-track minds!" Twinkles said crossly. "That's what everyone says. Look! Look at my Goddess!"

George and Tommy looked reluctantly at the Goddess.

"Perfect physical specimens," she said, looking back at them intently.

"We keep in shape," George said, slightly embarrassed by the close scrutiny.

A great wave curled up in the sea, far behind the Goddess.

"Sheez, Tommy, check that tube," George said urgently.

"Sweet!" Tommy exclaimed, as the wave thundered down into the sea like a fountain of white foam. The men looked at each other, and ran into the surf with their surf boards. In a minute or two they were quite far out in the water.

"They have no interest in - anything else?" asked the Goddess, looking a bit sad.

"Not when the surf is good, "Twinkles replied.

"Do they derive sensual pleasure from that?" the Goddess asked, strangely. "Does it make them feel happy?"

"Yes, I think so," replied Twinkles.

The Goddess gazed curiously at the men as they swam strongly in and out of the waves. She shrugged and then turned to Twinkles and smiled. A delicious dimple appeared at one side of her mouth, and her teeth shone whitely against the deep pink of her lips.

"What do you find pleasure in?" she asked.

Twinkles thought for a few seconds, and then she answered, "Oh, you know, shopping and dancing and clothes and music and everything, and maybe looking at Mike..."

The Goddess looked startled. "Shopping? Never heard of it. Music and clothes? "she enquired. "Then dancing and so on? And why do you like looking at Mike?"

Twinkles remembered that the Goddess could read minds, and she felt shy. "He hasn't really noticed me yet," she confessed, nibbling at one of her finger nails.

"Perhaps he is interested in other things as well?" asked the Goddess, and she added "How very peculiar".

"I suppose he is interested in lots of things," answered Twinkles, "Like video games..."

The Goddess repeated loudly, "Video games?" Then she looked closely at Twinkles.

Twinkles stood with her feet slightly apart, thumbs hooked into the top of her bikini bottom. The sea breeze blew strands of blonde hair around her neck; the red bandanna that was her bikini top was wrapped around her forehead, above her clear blue eyes and delicately arched eyebrows.

The skin on her body, bare above and below her bikini bottom, was soft and smooth.

The Goddess sighed, and looked as though she was about to say something else but was interrupted by George as a wave carried him to her feet. He showered her with droplets as he jumped up athletically. "Crunchers!" he shouted oddly, and with a faraway look in his eyes, he threw himself and his board back into the sea.

"He must be very old," the Goddess said as though working something out. "Much older than you are?"

"Well yes," said Twinkles said, "I think he's about twenty."

"Is that all? But of course, it's all different here," the Goddess mused. And she added, as though trying to explain, "We are much older than that. And we are not interested in other things. We have what you call one-track minds". And then she asked, "What do you think about me?"

Twinkles felt surprised, as that was such an odd question. She answered, "I was frightened at first, but now I think that you are quite nice, and you are very beautiful. I wish I looked like you".

The Goddess looked extremely surprised. "Well, that's very confusing. So, you're a pre-female. If you want to look like me, why don't you?" she asked.

And then Twinkles looked surprised. "Maybe I will, when I'm grown up. But it takes a long time to grow up," she said. "It takes ages and ages. We can't just think we're grown up".

The Goddess answered, "On the planet where I come from, we grow up very quickly and look like this when we want to. There are many who look like me. We are all very beautiful and not interested in anything like surfing and dancing. We can just imagine wearing different clothes, and then we are dressed in them".

"That's why you don't understand shopping, "said Twinkles. "It's interesting looking around the shops sometimes, and finding what you want".

"It sounds boring," said the Goddess. And she lifted the round box to her lips and said, "I have more information. The initial contact is a young specimen, who will grow into female shape eventually, but it takes a long time. Two older male specimens are perfect physically, but they were more interested in surf than in me. All three beings are interested in a range of activities, while our focus is on insalucidating". She put the round box to her ear, and then to her lips and answered, "All I know is that time is of the essence. We must start selecting as soon as possible. Durban may not be the right place, there are too many things - like looking for crunchers and barrels - for them to do here. We need a stronger focus".

"What are you selecting for?" asked Twinkles, when the Goddess had stopped talking into the box..

The Goddess answered, "We've got a shortage of male specimens on our planet. There was a law passed long ago banning games - like the old footie and ruggy and cricky - and drinking, so that we females could have their undivided attention. But they seem to get bored . Imagine that, surrounded by beautiful women and nothing else to do, except a little light housework, and they get bored! So we have to look for new males".

"Oh," said Twinkles, who thought that all sounded weird. But she knew that adults did strange things, whatever planets they were from, and asked, "So what do you do with the old males?"

The Goddess looked a bit annoyed. "Well, they eventually ask to go back to their own planets, and when they have become uncooperative and cease to function, we give them a spacecraft and let them go. In fact, they often cheer as they leave us, then sing rude songs about women who won't let them drink or play games. They often leave in a state of arousal, which is most insulting! Anyway", she concluded, "It looks as though Durban males may not be suitable".

Twinkles said helpfully, "Why don't you go to Jo'burg? It's bigger, and there are more men there. They have gold and diamond mines in that area".

"Too busy, too much there for them to be interested in," replied the Goddess, looking at her. "We want them to be interested in us". Then she said into the round box, "What about that small inland town that we mentioned earlier? The place with the good vibes, only a few shops, no television reception, and very little else? They play a game or two, and drink, but as we are beautiful and different, they will be content and manageable for some time." She listened to the box, and then said into it, "Agreed".

"Who are you talking to with that ?" asked Twinkles.

"To my crew", the Goddess replied.

"Do they have tentacles?" Twinkles asked.

"No," shuddered the Goddess, "they all look like me. They are all female forms. As I've explained, we have come here to build up our male stock, so we have to find willing specimens".

"How will you do that?" asked Twinkles.

The Goddess looked thoughtful. "It won't be too difficult, with the young being," she said, "In a place where there is no television and nothing much to do". She looked thoughtful and smiled. "We will take them by surprise".

Then she said, "Goodbye. Thank you for your input. It has been interesting to meet you, and to learn that you are a young pre-female. I thought at first that you were a pretty male child. Slivaak". Her sparkling dress disappeared, and the Goddess was clad in the blue wet suit as before.

She stood for a moment, all warm curved softness, then slid into the water. A second later, an enormous multi-coloured bubble rose out of the sea and hovered over Tommy and George. They looked up in astonishment, then abandoned their boards and swam hurriedly towards the shore and Twinkles, sending small plumes of disturbed water into the air.

In the bubble-craft, the Goddess changed her wet suit into a white uniform with a very short skirt, like the rest of the crew, then bent her head as she listened to their thoughts. "They are very primitive, "she said out loud. "They have never seen spacecrafts like ours before, and it frightened them!" The Goddess and the crew were amused. "But strange things give them pleasure, so while in this world, we must not," she added seriously, after a few seconds, "Do as they do. We must not become interested in other things, or start to watch television, or want to play games. Those things seem to be infectious. Oh yes, and there is an urge to do a thing called shopping. I will explain what that is, as we proceed. Now, what is this small town called that we are going to? I must encode it into the planet-nav".

❖ The bubble accelerated upwards at a great rate. Tommy and George stood next to Twinkles on the sand, watching it. "Way out", George breathed.

The bubble disappeared, and became part of a tiny white cloud in the blue sky. The cloud changed into strands of silver that drifted down into the sea.

"Far out", Tommy agreed.

Twinkles sobbed.

George's eyes focussed on her, at last. "What's the matter?" he asked kindly. "Are you frightened?"

"No", cried Twinkles, "She didn't know that I was a girl! She said I was pretty, though. I want to be grown up and look like the Goddess".

"You don't want to grow up too quickly," said Tommy. "In any case, you're a gorgeous young chick. You'll be much better looking than her when you're older. You're only a kid, you've got plenty of time".

George looked at her, and said, "You'll be okay in a few years, better than ok. You won't be able to wear your bikini on your head then. Sheez, you remind me of my little sister. She's a nut, too".

And Tommy added, "That was so weird! We were talking to a space being. There was a UFO! Nobody will ever believe us." Then he looked at the sea, and shouted, "George, the tide's turned!" And abruptly, George and Tommy grabbed their boards that were bobbing around in wavelets near the beach, and ran back into the sea.

Twinkles watched them as they swam out through the surf. Then she smiled.

She slowly unwound the bikini top from her head. "A gorgeous young chick," Tommy had said. She smiled again as she wrapped the bikini around her flat chest, and tied it into place. Shading her eyes with her hand, she looked up into the sky. There was no bubble to be seen, anywhere in the sky. She turned and started to jog homewards along the beach, with the breaking waves bubbling and foaming on the sand.

"Mum?" she asked later, when she got home, and raced into the sitting room where her mother was sitting reading. "Mum? Do you reckon I'm a gorgeous young chick, and do you believe in beings from outer space?"

"Yes, you silly old gorgeous Twinkle-toes", her mother replied," You are so pretty. And maybe there are beings in outer space. Why do you ask, Twinkles ?" She closed the book, "Teenagers, and How to Cope with Them", and looked earnestly at her daughter.

"I'll tell you later, but that's another thing," Twinkles said. "I think that, as I am growing up, you must call me by my proper name".

"Okay, Erica," her mother said, looking a bit sad, but then she exclaimed, "Oh! Before I forget, Mike rang and said to tell you that it's not an indoor party tonight, it's a shorts and T-shirt party on the beach".

Twinkles remembered fleetingly the unproductive shopping trip and the depression of the T-shirt rail, and it ceased to matter. "Love you, Mum," she shouted, halfway to her room, and the flowery newish shorts and newish T-shirt that would be perfect for a beach party.

Twinkles' mother smiled and went back to reading her book .

"I am so, so happy," Twinkles though loudly. She thought it so loudly that a craftful of phenomenal-looking Goddesses, who were still tuned in to the Durban frequency, winced as they turned it off. They were about to land in the small town with good vibes, and the distraction was unwelcome. They turned the new frequency on, and listened to it hopefully .

"This has got to be one of the best places we have ever been to when selecting new males! Just listen to what they are thinking!" one of them said, as their craft bubble settled gently onto a mine-dump. "They really need us here! They will be happy when they see us coming!"

"Oh yes," another agreed, and she added, "It won't take us long to persuade them to come with us!"

Slivaak!" they called softly, in their tuneful voices, and clad in soft silver dresses that clung to their divine bodies, and floated like cobwebs about them, they stepped out into the receptive air.

It was hot and sweet, hot and sweet.

SWEET MEMORIES

From the highway, Johannesburg looked like a piece of modern art. Structures of different heights, widths, and textures, raised varying colours into a deep blue sky. There were tiny parched yellow patches of grass near the edge of the road. There were no trees here. It was a surrealistic view, but there was no great poinsettia flower with tears like diamonds on its petals, floating on a crimson cloud in the sky, as there might have been on a canvas. If there had been a poinsettia in the sky it would have been burning, because the sun was so hot. It was Christmas Eve. The last bit of Christmas shopping was in the car boot.

It was hot, cruelly hot, in the car. The dashboard was too hot to touch. The poinsettia would have been painted the hottest red imaginable, I thought. The painter leant towards me, his face bristling with passion. "And now, you beautiful woman, now that I have completed one work of art, I will start on another. Come to me, my love, so that I can paint you...".

"Knock knock," Robert said.

"Who's there?" Simon asked.

"Soup".

"Soup who?"

Robert giggled. "Superman!" he shouted.

The traffic moved smoothly. I changed into fourth gear. Blue, blue eyes. They were super. I looked into a man's blue eyes, and saw the intensity of his longing. He touched my cheek with a gentle, caring hand and said, "My darling, I never thought I could love anyone as much as I love you". My heart started to pound as I knew exactly how it would feel when we kissed. His caressing hand moved from my cheek to my neck, and I knew how good it would feel when we held each other. I reached out for him, and....

"Bloody hell!" I said in surprise, in answer to a knocking sound coming front the front left tyre.

"Don't swear!" the twins said together.

"Sorry guys," I said to my sons, "We've got a flat tyre".

We stopped on the yellow verge, and an endless stream of vehicles flashed past us, like the noisy torrents of water rushing down the roads in the wet season. But there was no cooling rain, it was hot, too hot. The children climbed out of the open window, and helped me to get the jack and the tool box and the spare tyre out of the boot, from under the shopping bags. A car pulled over in front of us, and a man walked towards us. He looked surprised when he saw me.

"Hi!" he said. "Can I help you with the tyre?"

"Yes please!" I said, "Changing tyres is not my idea of fun!"

He grinned, and took the jack out of my hand. He had very blue eyes. "Come on, boys," he said to Robert and Simon, " I need some assistance here".

I sat on some yellow grass, and listened to the boys and the man chattering away about school, and spanners, and let my mind wander. The sun shone down. I lifted my damp hair away from the back of my neck. It was so nice not to have to do battle with the tyres! Thank goodness for kind people! There were not enough unselfish people in the world. Random acts of kindness were such a good idea: doing shopping for someone here, lending a listening ear there, or sewing a hem up for somebody, or cooking a meal, or changing a tyre... Maybe there would be a thunder storm later. The rain would wash the dusty road, and chase away the heat for a little while.

"Thanks, boys", the man said to the twins, as he put the flat tyre and the jack and the tool box back in the boot, "You were useful there, a big help".

"Thanks a million," I sad gratefully, as the boys climbed back into the car, "Happy Xmas!"

The man looked into my eyes a bit longer than was necessary. Strangely, he looked familiar now, and he smiled as though he was amused about something.

"Glad I could help," he said to me. And "See you, Santa's helpers! " he said to the boys, as he walked towards his car.

As I opened the driver's door and sat down on the much too warm seat, I smiled to myself. "Of course!" I thought, he looked familiar because he had the blue, blue eyes of the super man that I had been imagining earlier. That was it. Strange, but these things happen. Coincidence. "Let's go, guys," I said to the boys, and we rejoined the traffic river and its fast-moving current.

We would be home soon. Johannesburg spread itself out, up and down, over rocky hills, and here and there mine dumps gleamed yellow-gold in the sun. The twins chatted and read their books as I drove, but I felt suddenly alone. It happened sometimes, now that I was divorced. But of course, it's better to be single than in a marriage without love or friendship.

When I was young, I had lots of friends. And Johannesburg itself was to me not just a city, but a dear, friendly, mysterious being. My school friends and I used to walk around the streets, up and down hills, as far as we could go before it got dark. We explored the streets and the parks, and the patches of grass, and trees, and rocks, and met many people. No two places, and no two people were the same! We knew all the best places to sit and chat, and all the kindest and most interesting people to visit. Some lived in great houses with two or more cars parked in the driveways, and some lived in little shacks with stones on the corrugated iron roofs to stop the sheets blowing away. We knew little spruits, or streams, where we could paddle, caves we could sit in and wonder at, and places high up on the mine dumps where we could sit and watch oblivious people passing by below.

As young teenagers, we could walk anywhere in Johannesburg at night. It was a safe place then. It was as though the city was the same age as us, and we were beings looking for happy adventures. We grew at the city's speed, as though it encompassed us, and we were part of its slow and steady pulse. But the city seemed to grow away from us as we grew older. It changed and withdrew from us, as we did from it. The safe and cosy relationship that we once had, had gradually disappeared, and left us feeling like we did with our families, like strangers who had to find other things to love. The comfort of the warm evenings when we had belonged together, had gone. We were like lovers left without love. We had given ourselves to the city and instead of a continuing warm embrace, it had left us with mere inanimate buildings. We had grown away from each other. And gradually our band of friends dwindled as they grew up and chose careers, worked hard at their studies, and went their own ways.

And now, years later, here I was, driving home with my beloved children but without a partner, a twin soul. I was incomplete, and I needed a close friend, the closest of true friends. I needed a lover, and his hard warm sweetness, and the safety I would feel with his body next to mine during the star-studded Johannesburg nights.

Later, when we were home, I stood looking out of the window. During the day, the panoramic view of rocky hills speckled with houses, trees and rocks, was beautiful. The boys sat at the dining table, playing with Lego. Robert glanced at the clock, and said, "It's still early, Mom, let's go up the kopje".

As I drove us to the kopje, I thought back to the happy times I had spent there with my friends. The hill, not far away from where we lived, had always been a favourite haunt of mine when I was young. There were a group of rocks there that my school friends and I thought of as our own. Families of small harmless lizards lived there, and sometimes left jumping tails behind them when they were disturbed and swiftly ran off. When we were children, the rocks became castles and ships, and much more besides, and when we were older, they became club-houses and meeting places. And sometimes, when we were teenagers, Freddy and I would climb up to sit and hold hands on our special rock. It was a large rock, the highest one. Freddy always said that it was his. After he and his family moved away from Johannesburg, nobody ever sat there again. I missed him a lot, and we wrote to each other for a while, but we were young and the letters eventually stopped.   Freddy. His eyes were so blue...

"It was Freddy!" I said out loudly, in surprise, "I went to school with him!"

Robert said, without looking up, ""Yes, he told us while he was changing the tyre".

"Did he really?" I asked, "Well, why didn't he say anything to me?"

"He said lots, Mom," Simon answered, "But you were probably day-dreaming away, and didn't listen.   You do that sometimes".

"Oh dear," I said.

I parked the car, and we walked in the twilight through the dry grass towards the rocks.   Johannesburg hummed with life around us in the near distance, but it was quiet here.   There were rustles as a few small creatures scuttled away from us.   We must have seemed like giants to them!   The warm night was soothing after the heat of the day.   We climbed the hill and sat down on a flattish rock, which Robert and Simon always chose as it was comfortable and we had a good view of the city from up there.   At night, lights sprang up now and then, quite slowly, then faster and faster, till the hilly city was a mass of light.   It sparkled with life and romance, like millions of diamonds.

We spoke about school, and holidays, and Christmas, and Simon said that Jesus must have enjoyed being born in a stable surrounded by friendly animals.   "And hay smells delicious," Robert agreed.

"I wonder which star guided the three wise men?" Simon mused, and we looked up from the lights on the hills to the stars which were becoming clearer in the night sky.   I gasped as I looked down again and glimpsed the figure of a man on the topmost rock outlined against the dark blue sky.   My heart missed a beat or two.   "It's Freddy, Mom," Simon said.   "He said he would meet us here".

"Sorry if I startled you," Freddy said as he joined us.   "I couldn't resist going up to my very own rock again!   We spent quite a bit of time up there, didn't we," he said to me, smiling.   He sat down next to me, and his knee touched mine.   Being next to him felt the same as it had, all those years ago.   I felt secure, as though a missing part of me had been returned.

We four sat there, that Christmas Eve, and talked comfortably into the night.　　Cars raced here and there in the city that sparkled below us, and the bands played, while people danced and ate and drank, and streamers flew through the air in bright colours.　　We sat on the centuries-old rock, on the kopje, while bubbles of merry-making sounds floated towards us on the warm city air.　　Freddy's hand felt right in mine,　as though we had both come home, and we were back in the place where we belonged.　The empty space that I had lived in for too long, had filled up with a loving, familiar feeling.

Much later, after we had parked the cars at my house, and the children were asleep in their beds, we arranged their presents carefully under the decorated tree.　　After that, we made cups of coffee and while we drank it in the sitting-room, we chatted about what we had done since we were young, and had last seen each other.　Then Freddy said, "We've been apart, we've learnt a lot about life, and like you I've been divorced for a while, but I've always known what I most wanted".　He took the cup gently out of my hand, put our cups on the coffee table, and turned to me.　"I want you," he said," And I want to kiss you now!" And he put his arms around me and pulled me towards him, and he kissed me, and kissed me again, and he was what I had always missed and always wanted.

"It's very late",　he said, "I'll see you tomorrow".　And he drove off into the night.

In the morning, Robert and Simon tore the wrapping off their presents, shouting excitedly.　The city traffic hummed into the daylight. The city had never been asleep, it had just been waiting for this special day.　It was already hot, so hot, and the sun streamed in relentlessly through the open window.　On the kopje, lizards sun-bathed on the old, warm rocks.

"Knock knock", Robert said, fitting some model railway tracks together.

"Who's there?" Simon asked, putting glue on the piece of a model aeroplane.

"He".

"He who?"

Somebody real knocked on the front door.

"He-man!" Simon said, and they both giggled.

But I knew that it wasn't he-man or a super-man who had knocked on my door and come home at last. It wasn't an imaginary man, he was my real man. He came with Christmas, and its promise of a new beginning. I opened the door and looked into his blue eyes.

"I missed you," we said together, and we both laughed with happiness.

"Happy Christmas", I said.

"Happy Christmas", said Freddy, and it was, and it always will be, now.

JANE

The child sat on the gate with her father, pressing her face against his rough jacket. She was secure. He told her stories about animals, and the field of wheat before them shimmered with small creatures that danced among the stalks. Mice wearing boleros, crickets with flutes, and an assortment of tiny beings played and paraded before her. She gasped and watched, and after some time she became aware that her father's voice had stopped. So she told him what she had been looking at, and he laughed and said, "What an imagination you have! I'll tell you one thing, my precious child, you will never find life boring!" And she nodded, because she knew that he was always right. To her, he was as old as Rumpelstiltskin, and as wise as an owl.

It was war-time then, and I knew nothing about the war. I was asleep in my aunt's cottage in Derbyshire when the bomb fell late one night on London, and my beloved father was killed. My mother had died when I was born, and my aunt said that my parents were now happily together in distant Heaven. She said that I should not grieve so much, as we would all meet again one day, and that she would look after me till then.

Aunt Ethie was indeed good to the child, the little girl who was so aware of her loss, and who took refuge in daydreams too often at first. But time passed, and there was school, and then college, for Aunt Ethie and her niece. They did well. They had fun at times, and won prizes like the two leather-bound story books here on the book-case by my side. I don't know why I've kept them so long, but perhaps they help me to identify with the child that was me. I can look at her as though observing someone else entirely. I feel for her, but she isn't a part of me. Aunt Ethie's orphan isn't really me at all. Because, when I reach deep into my mind, there is such a happy childhood there! We sang and romped in the sunlight, and snuggled together, giggling, when the weather was cold. We were adored, I know, but never spoilt. There never was such a happy family! That's what I remember most of the time. I wasn't lost and alone like the child that Aunt Ethie had taken in and looked after.

I was completely alone in the world when Aunt Ethie died. I had truly loved her. So, in an effort to leave the pain of loss behind, I moved away from where we had lived, and settled down here in this house. There are gentle hills and pretty fields around me, unlike the windswept wildness of the scenery that I had known before. The house is attractive, and not too far from the town and the office. It was quiet here at first, with Dr. and Mrs. Henderson, my nearest neighbours, a fair distance away. But all that changed when they began to build Jane's house in the field opposite my house. Up till then, the evenings and weekends had been too uneventful. I sometimes felt that the hills were getting closer, and would surround me like an enormous grassy cage. And I would escape, gasping, to the Hendersons, for a chat. They were always most welcoming, a charming couple. But then the new house provided so much interest for me that I stopped seeing them so often.

I would note happily, on my arrival home from work each evening, another few layers of brick-work, or another section of timbering. And eventually, Jane's house was completed, and the family arrived.

What a difference it made to have that family so near me! Of course, three children seemed an immense crowd to me at first. The two older boys would run around their house shouting and laughing and playing rough games, but they never annoyed me. I grew to like their excitement and happiness, and noise. And it wasn't long before I got to know Jane, and the baby.

Babies were almost unknown to me, and I delighted in the new experience of having one nearby. He had a cloud of blonde, fluffy hair, and sparkling brown eyes. He was adorable, and I could have played with him for hours. And then there was Jane. She was, I thought, perfect. Her pretty face seemed alive with love and reassurance. She looked after the children so well, and they and the neat new house reflected her care. Her husband was a shadowy figure, but I saw him kiss his wife with great tenderness before he left for work each morning. And I would glimpse him each weekend, as he played with the boys, washed his car, or tended the garden. They seemed ideally happy, all of them, and as close as families should be.

The oldest child, Simon, became a particular friend of mine. My father's name had been Simon, too, and it gave me such happiness to say his name out loud. Simon would appear whenever I most needed him, like the time when I had a pile of documents to get through, and a migraine that made work impossible. He helped me to make a cup of tea, and reminded me to take my pills. Then, later, when my headache had receded, I could read to him again from one of my old story books. He was a wonderful person, that small boy. He was a lot like his mother. Jane, my Jane, was such a comfort to me. Her presence calmed me, and made me feel capable of anything again. She always looked fresh and composed. She had great beauty of soul.

Sometimes, we would picnic in the countryside. The children would explore small streams and clumps of trees while the baby smiled and cooed beside us. We would talk of many things, and watch the clouds form fantastic shapes in the sky above. The wind would tug and blow them into castles and daffodils, ships and butterflies, and we would watch them and dream away, and later talk again. Jane's clarity of thought often surprised me. It reminded me of when I was young and idealistic, and the future looked as though it could be enchanting. Jane's hair was the same colour that mine had been before the greyness began. I knew that Jane and her family were all that I had ever wanted. I knew that I would never feel lonely again. I was completely happy.

I seemed to work in a dream-state at the office, longing for the reality of my house. I had Jane and the family to go home to now!

Jim and Elaine Henderson dropped into the office one day, saying that they had missed my visits to them, and that they were concerned about me living in such an isolated spot. I laughed as I thanked them. "I have so much to keep myself occupied with, nowadays!" I said. And they said how pleased they were that I was fine. When they left, I felt suddenly anxious and uneasy. That evening, that terrible evening, Jane came running to my house. "Darling, don't be too sad", she said to me, "I am sad, but you mustn't be. You see, we have to go".

"Go? Away?" I asked nervously, "Why?"

"Well, my husband has been offered another job, more money, and we think that it will be better for us all", she answered, her eyes shining with tears. "I've loved my house, and - and you, so much. I never had a family as a child, and you somehow filled that gap in my life. I want you to know that".

I could hardly trust myself to speak. "I know. I feel the same about you. I'll miss you all so much. Especially you, my dear".

Her lips brushed my cheek, and her perfume - that clear scent that reminded me of solitary walks in the dewy grass of summer - surrounded me. And then she was gone, back to her family. She would always have them, but I would have nothing if they left.

I couldn't go to work the next day, and felt sadness hanging over me like a grey cloud. I couldn't eat anything. I felt suffocated, and even glanced out of the window to see if the hills were closing in on me again. Jane's house was quiet, although Simon and his little brother appeared once at the front gate to blow a kiss or two in my direction. I was alarmed at the depth of my feeling for them, and for their family. What could I do? I waited, knowing that something would happen. I felt so desperate and afraid.

In the late afternoon, I heard a knock on the door. "Yes?" I called faintly, thinking that Simon had brought me a bunch of wild flowers, as he had done so often before.

I was surprised to hear Jim Henderson's voice, and I couldn't hold back my tears as he came into the room.

"They're going", I sobbed, "Going. And I don't know what to do".

Jim pushed aside some clothes and plates, and made room for himself to sit down on the sofa beside me. "What is going?" Jim asked, "Tell me what's wrong".

"Jane and her family. My precious Jane," I replied, feeling the tears drip down my cheeks. But at the same time, I felt comforted with him there. He was such a solid man, so down-to-earth, and real.

"Jane", echoed Jim. And then he added, "Elaine and I were worried about you when you stopped your visits to us, and even more so when you implied that you couldn't be lonely here. Tell me about Jane. Tell me why you are so unhappy, Janine".

"Jane has been everything to me," I said. "I can't let her go! I could have been like her, Jim! Her family could have been mine. I love them all so much. I even love their house!"

Jim put his arm around me. "Which house?" he asked, "Where?"

"The house opposite, of course," I said. "I watched it grow. It's Jane's house".

"Dear friend," Jim said slowly, "My dear Janine, look out of the window and tell me what you see".

And I looked out of the window, and the neat house, Jane's house, was there. And my family was there, my own family, the family that I should have had, the only family that I had in the world.

Then I looked again, and the house vanished, and the long grass and dandelions waved at me from the deserted field.

REFLECTIONS OF JOY

I sit here, looking into the mirror, and I wish I could tell you how kind he was, and how happy he made me, but I can't. I wish I could tell this story in another way, but if I did, it would be a lie. I told myself for years that the scar near my right eye, where he hit me and the gold ring on his finger cut into my flesh, fitted into the pattern of my laughter lines.

Laughter lines they're called, but mine are partly crying lines, though I have always tried to laugh as often as I could. We have to laugh, we have to tell ourselves that life will get better, we have to have hope.

He wanted the mirror in a dark corner of this room when he was here. It only reflected the dark corner opposite. Perhaps that was a symbolic representation of our life together. Now, I can move the mirror to wherever I want to, so that it reflects the trees and plants from the garden outside, and brings their beauty and graceful changing forms into this once joyless house.

That's what we're here for, isn't it, to look for joy and spread it where we can. To spread it thickly, like butter and honey on new bread for the children's tea. I always wanted children, but he said that a child would tie us down. And time went by, and then it was too late to have a child. So I kept working at his office, for him. I found him replacement secretaries once or twice, but he said they were never keen enough, cost too much money, and were only interested in themselves. He said that

I owed it to our customers to keep working there, even though I was not the best of secretaries, and he often complained about my stupid mistakes. But I knew the system, and the customers were my friends. When he was out of the office, I would chat to the customers about their lives, and we would spend a bit of time talking and laughing. When he was in, chatting was out of the question, as I then had to be as businesslike as possible. After all, as he said, we had to earn money, and he had a business to run.

After work, we kept ourselves to ourselves, as he preferred, and I learnt to become a really creative knitter. He was not keen on the radio or television, so he read his books while I knitted. I was not a good knitter, as my efforts sometimes made him smile or frown, but I was a creative one. It was a prosaic life, but to balance that, I fashioned the garments in the brightest of colours. Soft strands of wool can be knitted up into joyous forms. Powerful and radiant blues, reds, and purples, and the colour orange, reverberate with the magic of a scented summer's day. To me, though, orange is alive with a vibrancy and rhythm of its own.

When my brother John, a doctor, who had lived and worked overseas for years, moved back to this country, my husband kindly let me have an afternoon off so that John and I could meet and talk. John had found a job in the next town. It was good news! It was a joy to me to have my only relative, my dear brother, nearby at last. When I showed him my knitting, the shawls and cardigans, toys and pom-pom hats, he raised his eyebrows and said, "Even a doctor can tell that you are about to leave your husband, and will open a shop in Newcastle with all this stock. Or perhaps you will become a travelling knitwear merchant in the Himalayas?" I laughed, and John hugged me. "There's a possible option or two there," he said, and I nearly told him that I wasn't happy. But I couldn't spoil his home-coming, so I changed the subject and we talked about other things. I always wondered how much he guessed.

John hugged me again before he left. He said," We must get together every couple of weeks for a chat and perhaps a meal?" I said that it would be nice during times when the business was quiet, and we had less work to do. "Well, let me know, I have looked forwards to seeing you as often as possible, sister, now I'm home!" he said. Then he added with a small sigh, "I just hope there are enough sheep being sheared per annum to keep you in wool."

John drove over for a couple of hours when he could, and we chatted about inconsequential things over a light lunch or an afternoon tea. My husband was usually too busy, but sometimes he would open the door and say, "Hallo, how are you?" in a businesslike way, and then leave us to it.

You see, you make your bed and you have to lie in it. Some of us make our beds with imaginative roses, then hurt ourselves on unanticipated thorns as the dream turns into a nightmare. Then we have to learn how to endure. We hide the bruises on our bodies with clothes, and we hide the bruises on our hearts as best we can.

I couldn't hide the scar near my right eye. Because his breakfast toast was slightly burnt one morning, he lost his temper and slapped my face, and the gold ring on his finger cut me. I told the doctor that I'd hurt myself on a cupboard door that I'd carelessly left open. After all, it was my fault that the toast was burnt. After that, he hit me sometimes, never too hard, just enough to bruise me a little. I used to think that his words - that I was old, that I was ugly, that I was stupid - hurt me more. But I couldn't stop loving him, and anyway I had nobody else.

The day after I had been cut by the ring, I couldn't go to the office, and sat listening to some cheerful music on the radio while I sorted out scraps of wool. Patches of colour knit up into the brightest of tea cosies, toys, and mittens. I turned the music off when I heard his key in the front door, and a few minutes later he walked into the room. He didn't look at my face with the stitches hidden under a plaster, as he said, "This is for you", and put a little silver -coloured box on the arm of my chair. After a time, I opened the box and found a brooch in the shape of a silver rose with a beautiful blue sapphire in the middle of the flower. There was a note which said only, "Sorry". I picked up the brooch, which seemed to transmit an energy, one of hope and love, to me. I looked at it for a long time, and although it emanated hope, my heart ached like my face did. I found a pen, and scrawled on the back of the note, "And my scarred heart cries with helplessness" . My writing was so bad, because of the tears, that the words were illegible. But I always remembered what I wrote then, on that day, because I felt more alone then than I usually did, and I had nobody to comfort me.

It was not too long, a couple of years maybe, after his return that John rang me. My husband had left the office on a short errand but had stayed out for hours. That was so unlike him. As he often said, his work was his life, and he begrudged any time away from it. When John said, "He's had a heart attack, Anna. I'll meet you in Ward B", I was not too surprised. The taxi arrived as I locked up, and we were at the hospital in the next town fairly quickly. But when we reached the hospital entrance, John was standing there, and he told me that my husband had just died. He had not been able to speak, he had left no message.

I could not believe that the life I had led for all those years, had ended so suddenly and without warning. Our life together, as I sat and thought about it, suddenly looked so meaningless and sad. And all at once, I decided that I could not forgive myself, and I could not forgive him, for tolerating a life without a tangible joy.

One cheerless day, not long after the funeral, a gypsy stopped me, stepping before me in the cold and windy street. "I have a message for you from your husband", she said urgently. I stared at her. She held a bunch of summer jasmine incongruously in her hand. The wind blew random strands of hair across her face as she spoke. "You are still not at peace. You still cannot forgive. Wait for the rune of joy, it will come to you", and then she smiled and added, "It will come to you like this jasmine does, with love". She was suddenly not there, as though the wind had blown her away like a golden autumn leaf. She must have disappeared into the crowd. I stood there in the cold street, people brushing past me in the cold wind, with a bunch of jasmine in my hands. Each flower was as tender as a lover's kiss, and imparted a joyous expectation. Then I felt a jolt of warmth, as though a strong shaft of sunlight streamed onto me, onto me alone, as the clouds above parted momentarily, and the wind stopped.

Time passed as I sold the business, and took on a mornings-only job in a quiet office to give myself something to do. One night, as usual, I couldn't sleep. I worked on a rainbow-coloured shawl that scattered its magical colours like jewels around me in the lamplight. It was a comfortable chair, and I had the television on to keep me company, but I could not find any comfort within myself. My marriage had been so incomplete. I had tried, but not hard enough, it seemed to me. He was right, I had been inadequate. He had been a fine looking man, once. He had once been part of a dream of mine, but which he had found impossible to share.

Then the television screen went blank, and music from an unknown source filled the room.

It was appealing music, music that held me in a sweet embrace, that soothed my mind. It had an intricate tune, and the clarity of a flute rippled above its lower melodious waves. I heard a laugh that may or may not have been familiar, and a rune, the rune for joy, dropped out of the air and fell without a sound, without a touch, without warning, onto the shawl. A humming bird appeared, and I was not surprised. It darted around me fleetingly, and I could feel the happy movement of its wings. Then the bird vanished, the music stopped, the television resumed, and the multi-coloured shawl shimmered. I picked up the rune, and it was warm and inviting.

I knocked on the surgery door, and John called, "Come in". He smiled when he saw me, and got up to hug me. "Hallo, Anna," he said. We both sat down, and he continued, "I've been a bit worried about you since you rang me earlier, but I'm certain that you haven't started to 'experience psychotic episodes', as you put it. So, what's the date? And my middle name? And the name of the Prime Minister? And where did you go to school?". I gave him the answers, and he went on, "Have you written any letters to those in authority later, complaining about the Martians?". I laughed, and he said, "You're not in danger of losing your mind, Anna. Strange things do happen, that the sciences cannot explain. You're still rational, you've had a hardish time of it, but so have most people, and some have had very sad lives, far more difficult than you have had. I worried about you, being a sensitive soul and married to that cold man, but you had to make your own decisions, and decide your own fate, as all of us have to do. Life is a strange voyage, isn't it.

But for those of us who look upon difficulties as challenges, there are compensations and opportunities for self-growth".

He looked out of the window, musingly. "Believe me, things will get better as time goes on. One day you will find someone who loves you as much as you love him, and be happy. You will find joy again, in yourself and in your life". He paused, then added," No longer the helplessness/ Of a scarred heart's cry/When the fire of a sapphire/Spirals in a magical sky". He blinked, and looked at me, embarrassed, as I gasped. "Lines of a poem I must have heard once", he said, "Romantic". Then my brother shook his head and laughed. "You're okay really, love. Keep on with your morning job, but get out more for a change of scenery when you can. Don't sit around at home by yourself too much". His eyes twinkled. "Here's a good question for you knitters, Anna. Does black wool only come from black sheep?" We both grinned and hugged, and I left.

I made a point of going out more over the next few days, and had coffee and tea and lunch and an afternoon tea with old customers of mine who had become friends over the years. But sometimes the memories folded around me like a smothering fog.

One evening I held the rune for joy in my hand, and I imagined that it moved slightly. I thought about my late husband. To the people who saw him at work, he would have seemed a charming, though busy, and businesslike, gentleman. But his hurtful words to me would buzz around in my head for far too long. So what had been the point of it all? Why had I allowed the marriage to continue? It was as though I had been tied to him. But of course, there was no excuse for my stupidity, and the unhappiness. He must have been unhappy, too? There had been some good times, but too few. He was nearly always remote and cold, like a bleak mountain topped with snow. I should have tried to find joyousness in life for myself, and for him, too. "Better the devil you know...", I would tell myself, and "the grass isn't always greener...". How futile, what a waste.

But that was not a healthy way to think, because the past was the past, and I had to leave it there. The past had gone, and could not be changed. I wasn't living that life anymore, I was in the present, in the now, and I had to concentrate on that fact. What had gone before had taught me a lot. So now I had to relish the present and be thankful for it, and find joys and happiness in it, and live each new hour with faith and hope. The rune seemed to move again, as I thought how strange it was, though, that my brother had known the words I'd scribbled down so long ago. Nobody could have read that emotional scribble, it must have been a coincidence, an oddity. I held the rune tightly, as it felt as though it would jump out of my hand, and I wished that I could find an everlasting joy, a joy that would touch my soul, and which I could share...

There was a howling of wind, and my hair streamed out behind me, but I felt only excitement. I was nowhere and I was everywhere in a vast nothingness. Suddenly, a blazing mass of blue drove into the darkness, like the fire of a giant sapphire. I felt like a young girl on a roller coaster, and I laughed into the noisy spirals of whirling energy. Then everything stopped. I had just shut my eyes to better experience the feeling of wild delight, when suddenly and without warning his arms held me, and they were gentle and strong.

"Darling, my darling, here you are at last", he says. He is terrifyingly ugly, and I flinch as he towers over me. "Why do you look like this?" I ask him. "Because of my actions, my decisions," he replies huskily. "It was our destiny, though, we had to work through that, and we both had to learn from what happened. Forgive me, please forgive me". He puts his hand so slowly, as he knows how afraid I had been of him, so slowly on my shoulder. His fingers are twisted and gnarled, like his face, but his touch is soft. "I will be with you in the future, and I will cherish you", he says earnestly. "Do you believe that?"

"I want to," I tell him, "But..." And I look into his eyes, which are warm and loving. There is no coldness left, and it is as though joy is reflected in them now. "Believe me, my love," he says, "No longer the helplessness /Of a scarred heart's cry/When the fire of a sapphire/Spirals in a magical sky. You have heard these words before, and now you can understand their relevance".

"I will often send you roses and jasmine to remind you of my promises," he says, his voice trembling. He puts his ruined hands to his dreadful face, and tears trickle between his fingers. He kneels before me, and I reach out towards his head. "I will show you love and joy next time, next time", he sobs. I touch his hair, and then I wake up in my chair, and find that I am crying, too. My tears are as refreshing as the cool softness of welcome rain drops on a hot and languid day. The fragrance of heavy crimson roses fills the room, and my heart is filled with love and peace.

I wake up the next morning forgiving us both, at last. Maybe we had chosen our destiny, our fate, and had chosen our life together. Maybe we had been powerless to change the course of our predetermined lives, and the pattern of our relationship. But that was in the past, which cannot be changed. It is time to live in the present, in the here and now, which is full of opportunity. I have breakfast, and I notice that today is the second of December. The air is crisp and fresh, and clear. My neighbour rings my doorbell. "Morning, Anna", she says. "My aunt in South Africa has sent me a big bunch of roses and jasmine. I'd like to give you half of them, there's too much for me. Would you like these?". I take the flowers she holds out to me, and stroke their delicate petals. "How kind of you," I smile, "They're beautiful". And I think, "All will be well".

I now know that the present time is a priceless gift, which should be used wisely. The past, with its challenges and tests, has gone. This day is a chance to start anew.

Now, I hold the rune for joy in my hand, and it seems to pulsate with the clarity of hope and love. I look into the mirror, into my eyes, and I feel as though I can look through them into the heart of my being, into my soul. It is peaceful and calm, thoughtful and amused. It reminds me of a tranquil sea, with flecks of orange sunlight sparkling on the surface of its deep blue expectant surface. And now, when I look into the mirror, I see only reflections of joy.

HIGH AS A KITE

The victim, Edith Emerald Smith, glanced nervously at the monster. There it sat, wings gleaming in the sun. Surely it was far too large to fly? She imagined it unable to take off, and hopping hopelessly towards its – their? – destination. Trembling slightly, she smoothed her graying hair, and turned towards the vultures again. The vultures – respectable middle-aged pillars of society that they were – waited with impatient expectation for her to speak.

"But you all know I hate flying!," she quavered at last.

"Now look," Bernard said slowly, with an obviously insincere smile, "It's the quickest way to travel, and we didn't want you to miss a minute of your holiday". Head vulture, or Edith's elder brother Bernard, looked towards his other two sisters for help.

Jennifer said crossly, "Stop complaining, Edith, we've all paid for your birthday present holiday and we just want you to enjoy it." Their rebellious youngest sister, Patricia, sighed heavily, raised her eyes heavenwards, coughed loudly, and lit another cigarette.

The in-laws fluttered with embarrassment. "Yes, for sure," said Jennifer's husband George, uncertainly. "Never mind, then," Marion smiled nervously at her husband Bernard, hands twitching at her bag. The handbag fell open, and she peered shortsightedly into it, rummaging with one hand. In the sudden silence, change clinked and papers rustled while Marion carried out her search. "Oh here it is!" she exclaimed at last, with great relief. She handed a small package to Edith. "It's with our love," she twittered, "Listen to the ticks! It's a travelling clock, to accompany you on your travels! We hope that it will be useful."

Edith looked down at the brown paper wrapping, smudged and torn slightly at one corner. It just didn't make sense to her, this whole thing. She hadn't wanted to fly, ever. She hadn't wanted a clock. What were they trying to do to her? It was very kind of them, but she didn't understand why they were doing it. They hardly ever even noticed her, except when she was needed to house-sit or help someone move house, or assist in some way. Her legs shook with fright as she thought of the monster, and how her family had maneuvered her into this situation. She put the little packet in her handbag.

It was difficult, but summoning her energy, Edith pulled herself together. "Yes, yes, of course, "she murmured, her lower lip quivering slightly. She looked around at the expectant faces. "Thank you so much, all of you," she said as gratefully as she could. "Thank you for the holiday and the 'plane trip and the lovely clock." The family glanced at each other swiftly, and became animated once more.

"Have a nice holiday," Marion said, while pecking her lightly on the cheek. "Yes, do," said the others, patting her arm and kissing her gently. "Goodbye, dear Edith, goodbye." And Edith tottered, mesmerized, towards the aeroplane.

The monster quivered with what felt like malevolent life, as Edith glanced out of the small window fearfully. The family stood in a huddled group in the middle distance, while the airport buildings, rock-firm, towered behind them. Edith sat in the vibrations, her safety-belt's clasp reminding her of the various dangers that could lie ahead. If only there was some way of finding merciful oblivion, a suspended animation existence, while in the bowels of this unnatural flying contraption. She looked around at the other passengers in the 'plane, all chattering excitedly, laughing, and flicking through the pages of glossy magazines with nonchalant hands. The large handbag on her lap reminded her of the travelling clock, and she grimaced at the thought of the airborne hours, minutes, and seconds ahead, and the catastrophes and dramas that time could hold.

The monster rumbled crossly down the runway, and the other passengers became expectantly quiet. "The lull before a storm," thought Edith wildly, and then claustrophobia struck her with violence. Here she was, in the innards of this monstrous invention, with absolutely no way out. Then, as the aircraft rose into the sky, acrophobia clutched her, and she almost screamed. All that space below, and below that stood her family, all safe. She began to tremble violently, and a stewardess materialized to undo the enclosing safety-belt. "Could I have some water please?" Edith asked, then added," Actually I don't drink but maybe – er- an alcoholic drink?" The stewardess nodded and smiled impersonally and moved along the aisle, an unconcerned professional with no foreboding of impending disaster.

Edith sat rigidly, while blue sky and white fluffy clouds danced happily past her little round window. She finished paging through the booklet of safety instructions with a morbid curiosity and another empty glass in her hand. Feeling that to move her head slightly would be to rock the aircraft, and to stand up would result in a roll at the very least, she couldn't move, so she let her thoughts run wild. She felt like the only human being on the 'plane as everyone else laughed and spoke, ate and drank, like unthinking joyful zombies. She alone was aware of the recklessness of the situation now that the monster had them in its clutches and could do what it wished with them. If only she was still at the airport, feet planted solidly on the unyielding ground, and a gentle breeze ruffling her hair. And then suddenly, with no warning but a little cry of horror, she remembered the insurance.....

It was Bernard, the usually smiling dutiful older brother, who had wheedled her into that. "Tell you what, Edith," he had grinned sympathetically, "As you're so nervous, how about taking out an insurance policy? In the highly unlikely event of anything going wrong your nearest and dearest would be well provided for. But never ever forget that flying is the safest form of transport." Edith had stood there confusedly, in the hustle and bustle of the airport, and had eventually decided that it was a good idea. It would take up some of the long waiting time, as well. The family had all laughed and joked as she filled in insurance forms, saying that the airline wouldn't dare to be anything but ultra cautious as such a large amount of money was involved. How very clever, Edith thought, as she now looked down at the handbag on her lap.

Should she tell the stewardess that she had a time-bomb ticking away in a little packet in her handbag? And demand to see the captain? She imagined how neurotic that would sound. She imagined how absurd she would look, all twitching hands and wild-eyed, unlike the calm, controlled and sensible middle-aged lady that she was. While she sat and thought, she ordered another drink, and then another, feeling that if a relaxed aura of self-control could be manufactured by alcohol, it would appear almost as authentic as the real thing. She assured herself that she was not just drinking but she was thinking as well. But then thoughts started to race around uncontrollably in her mind. She suddenly felt confused. Why would the family want to get rid of her? It seemed so ridiculous. And how should she announce the time-bomb fact? Maybe in an accusing way that would denounce her whole family? Should she pretend that someone else had given her the little packet? Should she just stand up and scream so that everyone could hear? But she decided against that, as all the other passengers sounded so cheerful that she didn't want to upset them. No, she would have to declare the bomb first, and then when it was disposed of, she could say what she wanted to, and how things had happened. It seemed impossible, though, that her family would do such a terrible thing. She sipped at her drink, pondering. Vultures, that is what her family had reminded her of, at the airport. Was that a sign? Or was that because she had been thinking – maybe too much - of flying creatures? If so, why not robins or dragons? Vultures flapped into her mind again. She had to make sure that the insurance money would not fall into the wrong hands.

Edith took the little ticking packet out of her handbag and held it in her hand. With her free hand, she caught at the stewardess's arm as she passed her seat. The stewardess said, "I'm sorry, Madam, but there are no more alcoholic drinks available. Would you like a coffee?"

Edith found that her lips felt rather loose as she began to speak. "Sh- sh- inch – insurance. It wash for the vultures."

The stewardess said, "Never mind, Madam, I will get you a coffee."

Clutching the little packet, Edith struggled to her feet, as the 'plane seemed to fly through several air pockets at once. She gave the packet to the stewardess and said carefully, "Please to open it," and then she fell in a heap on the floor.

"With our love, dear sister, from Bernard, Jennifer, and Patricia". The wreath lay on the new grave, its message clear. There were other floral tributes too, from the in-laws and friends. The funeral was over, and now only the immediate family stood there in the light drizzle. "I wish we hadn't done it," said Bernard mournfully, and Marion's fingers tightened on his arm. "How dare you," she hissed. "It was your idea!" Jennifer, her shoes muddied by the newly dug earth, looked across the grave at them. "Don't be stupid, Bernard, just think of the money," she said. "Yes," said George 'slowly', And no more dowdy, fussy Edith." Patricia blew a cloud of smoke towards them and coughed. "I'm sure that the loss of Edith and the money compensate adequately for the occasional twinge of conscience," she observed. They looked down at the grave, and Bernard laughed. "Of course, of course," he smiled. "Who's coming for a champagne and caviar breakfast?" he asked. They moved away, sated and content, like vultures. And all the while the drizzle fell like tears onto the wreaths, gradually seeping through earth, wood, and the tiny remains of Edith.

She could actually feel the drizzle! "Are you feeling a bit better now?" The stewardess asked, as Edith opened her eyes. "You must have fainted," she said, as she dabbed Edith's forehead with a damp cloth. "Let me help you into a more comfortable position in your seat, and after you have had a nap I will bring you a cup of coffee." She picked up a pretty little travelling clock from the next seat and put it into the top of Edith's handbag. "It was in a packet that you asked me to open just before you fainted. Isn't it lovely?"

"Lovely, lovely," repeated Edith, as she started to slip into the merciful oblivion of a somewhat alcohol-induced sleep. Just as the comforting hum of the 'planes' engines lulled her to sleep, Edith saw a cable in her mind's eye. It read, "To my dear family. You were right, the flight and the clock were delightful presents. With thanks and love, Edith."

SUMMER HOLIDAY

Roberta's chestnut curls were still tousled with sleep, but her brown eyes gleamed with mischief.

"Sit on my bed," she lisped, with three year old charm. Kathleen, almost five, looked at her warily for a few seconds, then Roberta held out her chubby arms pleadingly. Soon, the children were jumping on the bed, holding hands and laughing. Kathleen, panting with effort and laughter, collapsed suddenly, and Roberta began to pretend that she was a dog. "Woof, Kathleen, woof," she grinned, "Watch out!" She stopped jumping and sat down next to her sister.

Carefully, she lifted Kathleen's hand to her mouth, then her pearl-like white baby teeth bit sharply into her sister's flesh. Kathleen pulled her hand away, her grey eyes rounded in surprise.

"Don't cry, don't cry", begged Roberta, "Look – bite my arm". She held her small pink arm up, longing for the game to continue. Kathleen pushed the proffered arm away, and slid off her sister's bed. "No, I'm going to play alone," she said, and Roberta looked at her crossly.

"Play with me," she shouted, and began to cry noisily. As Kathleen left the room, Robert screamed loudly, and bit her own arm hard. She studied the teeth marks as she cried on, her eyes alight with tears and anger.

To Anne, the noise coming from Roberta's room was frightening. She pushed the newspaper across to Brian, who looked up from his book impatiently. "Do they have to fight on Sundays?" he asked crossly. Anne frowned. "Kathleen may be jealous of Roberta – oh, damn, I will have to go and look". She left the room hurriedly as Brian reached for his coffee cup.

"Kids," he muttered, then read on, engrossed again.

Roberta sobbed in her mother's arms as Anne stroked the little girl's hair. When the child was calmer, Anne sighed, and said, "Baby girl, you're better now. Tell Mummy what happened. Did Kathleen fight again?"

Roberta's baby mouth quivered. "See, Mummy," she said, holding her bitten arm up for her mother to scrutinise. Anne was horrified, and cuddled Roberta closely to her. She felt her small daughter's curls against her cheek, and the delicious plumpness of the small pyjama-clad body in her arms. She adored Roberta, who was such a loving and easily pleased, pretty child. She was so different to Kathleen, who was quiet and self-contained and plain. Anne sighed again, in exasperation, wondering vaguely how she could have produced two such different beings, such extremes. She became aware of the tangled sheets and blankets on the bed, and asked, "Have you been jumping on the bed, Roberta? You know that you shouldn't be doing that". Roberta, her eyes tearful, looked up at her mother. "Kathleen jumped, Mummy. Kathleen is a bad girl." "Yes, she was very naughty," said Anne. "I wish that she wasn't so disobedient." Anne knew what would follow: Kathleen's denials and stormy sobs, and more fuss and noise. Why, why, was that child so difficult? She gave Roberta a last hug. "Go and chat to Daddy for a little while, there's a good girl. I'm going to tell Kathleen what a naughty girl she is."

The baby Roberta heard Anne scolding Kathleen, and she smiled. Her pretty dimpled face was alive with pleasure. She was the good girl and nobody would ever be cross with her.

Kathleen rolled the shoes in newspaper and put them in the case. She turned towards the wardrobe, and her reflection gazed back at her from the mirror on the door. She was still too thin, and her feet and hands looked large and out of proportion on the tall, slight frame. Her dark hair was nondescript, pulled back off her face into a pony tail and unflatteringly arranged. She felt momentarily annoyed at the dullness of the reflected figure, and opened the wardrobe door quickly. She began to slip the few dresses off their hangers, folding them carelessly and placing them on the bed behind her.

Realizing that she was plain and that pretty dresses would look incongruous on her, she had never cared much for clothes. Roberta, now, had the looks to wear anything.

Kathleen suddenly remembered the red dress that Roberta had persuaded her to buy, and felt embarrassed. So much time had elapsed since then. Perhaps Roberta had tried to dissuade her from buying it? It was difficult to remember clearly, but she still felt ashamed...

The teenagers examined the dressed in the shop window. Roberta was charming today, and Kathleen was pleased that they were friends again. At home with their parents, there were so many misunderstandings that the sisters had little chance of true companionship.

Kathleen wondered sometimes if Roberta manipulated their parents, but then felt so guilty that she was unable to pursue that line of thought. No – Roberta was a darling, and she,

Kathleen, was clumsy, ungrateful, and disobedient. Kathleen knew that her parents preferred Roberta, and did not find that fact remarkable. After all, Roberta was so pretty and affectionate, and she, Kathleen – well, she wasn't like Roberta at all. Kathleen thought of the money she had in her purse, and felt remorse again because of the ideas she had about her family: the money was their present to her. It was her birthday, and she was to buy a special, expensive dress. "Come on Kath", Roberta urged, "Let's go in the shop now".

The shop was large and light, with rows of dresses displayed tantilisingly. Roberta flicked through a rail of garments with contemptuous hands. "No, Kath, I don't see anything," she said. Then, her face dimpling with pleasure, she said loudly, "Of course! The dress in the window!" Kathleen looked at her in dismay. "Which one? Not the red lace one? Oh no, Rob, it wouldn't suit me." "Rubbish!" Roberta cried, "You need something bright and cheerful. Try it on, silly".

It fitted, that dress, Kathleen thought, but did nothing else for her. Roberta said delightedly, "Gorgeous, Kath, super", and Kathleen looked at herself in the mirror again. The vivid colour made her skin look yellow, and the style just wasn't right for her. "It's terrible," she said flatly. "Oh Kath, you're such a fuddy-duddy, "Roberta pouted, "It makes you look marvellous. You're only seventeen, and the dress looks seventeen too." Kathleen smiled at her sister's words, and turned to face the mirror again. True, it did look smart, that dress; smart and frivolous. It fitted her, too... Roberta's shining curls were reflected for a moment in the mirror, and her bright, pretty eyes were warm. She looks admiring, Kathleen thought, she's admiring me. Perhaps I don't look too bad after all. "I'll take it," she said, "Thanks, Rob."

"Of all the stupid things to buy," Anne gasped. Roberta lifted a finger to her lips, urging her mother not to say anything else, while making sure that Kathleen didn't see her gesture. "She likes it, and I think it's lovely," Roberta declared stoutly. Anne thought, troubled, "Dear Roberta, defending Kathleen yet again". "Yes, yes," she lied loyally, out loud, "It is cheerful. The price horrified me at first..." Kathleen looked swiftly from mother to sister, turning so that the dress flared outrageously against her thin legs. "Oh, are you sure?" she asked doubtfully. "Anyway, I'll take it off now. I just wanted you to see it first, Mother".

As the door shut behind Kathleen, Anne gazed despairingly at Roberta. "It may be nasty of me, darling, but I sometimes think that girl may be – well – incapable," she said. Roberta said slowly, "Don't be hard on her, Mumsy. After all, she thinks she looks nice. Kathleen does strange things like this, as you know." She smiled, and crossed the room to sit on the arm of her mother's chair. "Let's just accept her as she is, shall we; she's barmy but harmless, poor thing."

Anne laughed at the pretty expression on Roberta's face, and patted her daughter's hand. You're so right", she said lovingly, "We have to accept her as she is, darling, dress and all".

When Kathleen had put her new red dress in the wardrobe, she felt oddly ashamed about it.

Her mother had been so cross about the dress at first. Everything she, Kathleen, did seemed to have unheralded repercussions. She remembered Roberta's look of admiration in the shop, and wondered fleetingly if it had been contrived. But of course not, she told herself guiltily. She had been grateful for her younger sister's companionship, and Roberta hadn't realised that maybe the dress wasn't quite right and a bit too dear. What a funny little sister, Kathleen thought, as she tried to smile.

Underwear went on top of the dresses in the case. Kathleen glanced at her watch as she walked over to the dressing table. Not much time for dawdling. She began to open drawers at random. Finding a jewellery box, she gazed at it before placing it beside a heap of small items and her hairbrush. "Reg," she thought, and then opened another drawer firmly.

"You're twenty-one," Roberta said, "You can do as you like. But honestly Kath you are mistaken." Kathleen looked at her, her face serious. "But Rob, just look at this jewellery box, it must have been so expensive." She held it out to Roberta, who took it and touched the curved lid as she spoke. "Men like that always give girls expensive presents. Don't you know anything? And it was Reg that I saw with that blonde girl -" She stopped suddenly and searched Kath's face appraisingly with her shining eyes. "Kath, I didn't want to tell you, but he had a simply beautiful girl with him in his car last night. As Paula and I left the cinema last night, they passed us. Paula was upset when I told her what I'd seen."

Kathleen stared at her sister wonderingly, and said, "But, Rob, he wants to marry me."

"Don't be so naive," Roberta said cuttingly. "I'll ask him about it," said Kathleen, "Perhaps it was his cousin?" Roberta sighed pityingly. "Of course he'll say he was escorting cousins.. Or that they were cases of mistaken identity, or he was out of the country at the time!"

She placed the jewellery box on her lap, and stretched out her graceful hands to her sister in despair. "Kath, listen, I'm your sister, and nobody else will be as honest with you. You're not exactly film star material, and you're not terribly clever either. But I love you and don't want you to make a terrible mistake. Oh Kath, can't you see what he wants? He wants a housekeeper, that's all, somebody who adores him and lets him do as he pleases. How degrading!" Kathleen thought wildly, "I'm nothing, I'm nothing," as tears ran down her cheeks. "I'm sorry, Kath dear, don't cry," said Roberta, "Shall I 'phone him and say you've got another boyfriend? Shall I? Rich and handsome? Who thinks the world of you?"

Through the coldness of her misery, Kathleen felt a small surge of warmth for her little sister. "Yes, ring him now," she said through her tears, knowing that she would never forget the sadness Reg had caused her.

Roberta, her hand on the telephone, looked at her parents. "I know," she had said, a worried frown on her face, "But Kathleen wants to break it off. She's in her bedroom and won't come out. She asked me to ring Reg and tell him." Anne snorted. "That stupid girl," she wailed," He's such a nice man too, and thought the world of her." Roberta said quietly,

"Well, she must have her reasons". Brian got up from his chair and went over to touch his daughter's cheek tenderly, knowing how upset she must feel having to make that call.

"What shall we do?" he asked. Roberta considered for a few seconds and answered, "Don't let's mention it again. I'll tell Reg what she wants me to. If she reconsiders, it's up to her. We don't want to be too interfering, do we?" She picked up the receiver, her face expressionless, and began to dial.

Everything was in, and Kathleen closed the lid. She looked around the room, feeling lost and afraid. But of course, Roberta had been right about her having to leave. Now that father had passed away, it seemed the most sensible course. Mother and Roberta would share a flat. Roberta had said, "Three women in one small flat would be too much, Kath, and anyway, you've turned out to be so independent and capable, and a good coper. You can find a good job and a nice bed sit now that we've sold the house and shared the money, and bought the flat. ""But will you manage the move and the packing?" Kathleen had asked. "Oh, you old worrier," Roberta had said, smiling. "Forget about the work. It will take our minds off you because we will miss you."

"I still don't understand it," Anne had sniffed crossly.

"Oh Mumkins," said Roberta, pleadingly, "Don't think she's abandoning us. I'm not leaving you as well". Anne, filled with alarm, had replied, "Don't ever say that, even as a joke!" "Am I too valuable to lose?" Roberta laughed, and Anne had replied seriously,

"Yes, you always have been. You know that. But I still think Kath should have stayed to help us with the move and deciding on the new furniture and which car to buy and everything. Too much to expect, I suppose, she never was a thoughtful person, like you."

And Roberta smiled radiantly. "You've got me, Mumkins, "she said.

Kathleen came into the room, her unbuttoned coat making her look more untidy then usual. "I'd better go," she said, "Or I'll miss the train. Take care of yourselves, and let me know if I can help you in any way". She hugged them both, and her mother kissed her fleetingly on the chin, and Roberta patted her arm. As she turned to go,

Roberta said, "One moment, old thing," and she buttoned Kathleen's coat with her smooth white hands. "You look much better now. Keep in touch! 'Bye!"

Kathleen stood on the platform at the railway station, and wondered if she would have an empty seat to herself on the train so she could cry. She thought of the warmth of the relationship that her mother and sister had, and wondered why she, Kathleen, had never fitted in, had never been cherished. But of course, people came with different personalities that sometimes clashed, and people wanted different things in life.... And of course she herself wasn't bright and bubbly like Roberta; in fact, she was plain and not very clever.... And then, as the train appeared, small and bustling, down the track, she thought of the way that Roberta had kindly buttoned her coat for her, and grief welled up inside her. She almost said out loud, "I'm going to miss them so much", but then she clutched the handle of her case more tightly, and stood up straight as the train drew to a stop in front of her. "I know what I'm going to do," she thought, "I'm going to pretend that I'm having an adventure. I'm escaping on a summer holiday by myself."

She smiled and, looking almost pretty, stepped into her holiday.

POEMS

Green Roses:
Once, in a Corner of My Garden in Southern Africa

Earlier, a chingalolo rested its many legs here,
A millipede in the rockery,
Curled up in a shining dark brown circle
Like an amber pendant;
But now, looking like soapstone carvings,
Between small patches of yellowing grass
And sun-warmed stones,
The succulents live alone.

They grow firm and oblivious to finger touch;
Their smooth green heads have thick petals
Like exotic plump and sturdy green roses,
And from the heart of each succulent
Stretches a thin green stalk tipped with tiny intricate flowers.

Some fading blossoms that, in their youth,
Dazzled like expensive and imported buttercup-yellow poppies,
Have dropped ochre ragged petals randomly
And, lying frayed with the delicate beauty of old age,
Poignantly add texture and colour, and a faint, beloved scent.
An exquisite memory from another time and place,
The picture is as firm now as it ever was,
Like a crafted work of art made of jade, amber, and old lace.

Ode to Secretory IgA

Coating epithelial surfaces to protect from invasion by micro-organisms,
You save my life even though I do not know you personally speaking.
Unknown yet kind and powerful
Tender and elusive as a passing summer night,
You care for me and the cells that are me –
Touch us, caress us, and you keep out of sight.

Why can I never greet you as an equal,
See you as just a friend?
Hold you as a lover, feel you as a sequel,
World now, without an end….

My inspiration; enigma surpassing; my IgA, my own:
You will leave me one day bereft and frail
To mighty germs, viruses like weeds so quickly grown,
And simulate a rainbow crock, a holy grail.

Unattainable – a glimpse of what one day
Could be a sparkling, prophesying ghost.
You live in me, my secretory IgA,
And I long for you, an entwined and lonely host.

Touchingly, To My Sons

Bubbles of milk scattered like stars,
and your soft warmness in the dark hours.
Although sometimes you tear at my face and yours,
indiscriminately.
Beautiful child, you are so familiar to me!
Your eyes glow and sparkle with intelligence
and remembrance.....

Did we share previous incarnations,
souls wandering together,
Ever to meet for a while, to serve ultimate
wisdom's pleasure?
Angelic smiles and tears; happiness and sadness
now as then.
Regretfully, I cannot shield you forever from
the winds of fate.

There Are No Hyenas in Salisbury

1

On hot and humid nights, and all the many others, I hear
the cries of the dead.
A dark-skinned child's hand, disembodied, with the pink
pleading palm uppermost.
A defenceless curl of blonde hair on the smooth and sun-burned
forehead of a teenage soldier.
Young and old, unlined and wrinkled skin, they form a
many-coloured shifting shadow about me.
And their wounds gape, with me forever.

2

They are history, those newly dead, and those who fell
as bloodily before.
Are they dead before their time, or did the Presence decree
that they should leave us here
To complete a glowing fragment of life's tapestry.
Perhaps karmic actions: lives ago, they killed and had to
be so, now.
White and black, child and adult; the shot, the stabbed,
the hacked, the burned, the mutilated,
When you drift into my mind, I weep for you and yours.

3

Your sighing and moaning may be the wind in the trees
or the distant, pre-dawn traffic.
There are no hyenas in Salisbury, to pick the bones from
the dustbins of the great hotels, the houses, but
What are these shadows? The flickering of lamps would not be
so eloquent, and would not show your faces.
Young man, old woman, and tiny child, I know you as well as I
know myself, and you are with me.
You move around me, I see you plainly – how do you support
yourselves, so torn and bloody -
I will never forget you.

Reflections on Poetry

At first, the epic dipped and flowed, occasionally meandered;
But never through waters defiantly defiled.
Then, fluidity and ripples, that some would call banality,
The essence now of sweetness, that seductively beguiled.
Without warning
Onto rocks of contrivance
To break starkly into pairs of muddy drops
Copulating
Near a sewage outfall pipe.
Later, the current moved heavily and free,
Towards scintillating waters and wakeful crimson depths.
Tomorrow, protozoa dance on ozone,
Anemones deliver forth jewels,
And the sand stirs upwards, revealingly.

Surprise Ending For Kojak And Mcgarrett

Superlative suits, and quick keen eyes,
Strong calm hands, and brilliant minds;
These fabulous men, intrepid guys,
Inspire we mortals of lower kinds.
Munching his lolly, hand steady on gun,
An admiring dolly, and "book him" when done;
Their legs can move faster, their minds are acute,
Their looks are so gorgeous, they're never scared mute.
To we homely viewers – oh Telly, oh Jack -
They epitomize hero: stiff lip and straight back.

Telly and Jack, though, not Theo and Steve:
The actors with T-shirts, no make-up today;
Would we feel admiration or stand there and grieve
If a maniac murderer stood barring their way?
Perhaps touched now with stubble, just fuzz on the pate,
Words all a-bubble, responses too late;
Maybe hair looking messy, mouths open in dread,
No camera, no script, and they're clean out of lead.
Taking aim – their actions heroic but quaint -
They have nothing to fire with but sticks of grease paint.